Stalker
By Anthony Uyl

Devoted Publishing
Woodstock, Ontario, 2017

Stalker
By Anthony Uyl

What kind of stories do you have?
Let us know!

Visit our website: www.devotedpublishing.com
Contact us at: devotedpub@hotmail.com
Visit us on Facebook: @DevotedPublishing

Published in Woodstock, Ontario, Canada 2017

For bulk theatrical rates, please contact us at the above email address.

ISBN: 978-1-77356-095-3

Act 1

INT. - DAD'S HOUSE – NIGHT

Sara comes running through the kitchen. She is frantic and has a phone in her hands. The front door blows open from the wind letting out an eerie squeek.

SARA:
(in phone)
Hello? Yes, hello?
(pause)
There's a man in my house.
(pause)
No, I don't know who he is.
(pause)
He's wearing a mask and carrying a knife.
(pause)
Please send someone.
(pause)
Okay, please hurry.

The sound of the front door slamming shut is heard and the sound of the lock turning resounds through the house.

SARA:
Shit. Please, whatever you want, just take it.

STALKER (V.O.):
I already have what I want.

SARA:
Then please just leave.

STALKER (V.O.):
But you haven't even heard what it is.

SARA:
Please, I beg of you just go.

STALKER (V.O.):
No.

SARA:
Please.

STALKER appears from around the corner of the front door. Sara screams and runs down a hallway towards the back of the house. She turns to look where Stalker is and hurries down the hallway to the bathroom at the end of the hall.

SARA:
Please no, please.

STALKER (V.O.):
But you still haven't guessed.

Stalker

SARA:
Guessed what?

STALKER (V.O.):
What I already have that I want.

SARA:
(crying)
Fine, what is it?

STALKER:
Why, my beautiful Sara, it's you.

Sara screams and a knife comes down and begins to stab her. Blood flows through the bathroom tiles as Sara falls to the floor twitching.

EXT. - SERENE CEMETARY – DAY

A group of mourners are gathered around a casket. It is situated in front of a gravestone.

INSERT – GRAVESTONE

On the gravestone it says, Sara Grayson, Born May 13, 1989, Taken To Soon.

BACK TO CEMETARY

SCARLET wipes away tears as MOM and DAD stand behind her. SAD MINISTER is speaking.

SAD MINISTER:
And though I walk through the valley of the shadow of death I shall fear no evil. For your rod and your staff they comfort me, all the days of my life.
(pause)
Feel free to pay your final respects.

Scarlet walks up to the casket and places a single rose on top of it.

SCARLET:
We'll get him Sara, I promise, we'll get him.

MOM:
C'mon baby, we'll get past this.

SCARLET:
I don't believe I ever will.

MOM:
You will. It'll just take time.

SCARLET:
She was my best friend.

MOM:
I know she was, but we'll be here for you.

SCARLET:
Who, you and dad? I was at school and not at Dad's with Sara. If I had been there this wouldn't have happened.

MOM:
If you had been there you'd be right there beside your sister.

SCARLET:
You don't know that.

DAD:
You're just upset. Please don't be mad at your mom.

SCARLET:
Don't defend her.

DAD:
This is just as hard for us.

SCARLET:
It doesn't seem like it.

MOM:
Believe us, it is. C'mon baby let's go home.

SCARLET:
I'd rather go with dad.

DAD:
You know that isn't possible. The police still have the house blocked off.

SCARLET:
Aren't they done looking for evidence?

DAD:
I'll call you when they're done.

Mom scowls.

SCARLET:
Fine.

INT. - SCARLET'S BEDROOM – DAY

Scarlet walks into her bedroom, sits on her bed and cries. She takes off her dress and puts on a sweatshirt and pair of track pants. She then walks out into the living room, sits on the couch and turns on the T.V. Mom comes in soon after.

MOM:
When did you want to head back to school?

SCARLET:
You're asking me that now?

MOM:
You're going to have to explain to your professors why you were gone.

SCARLET:
I'll get around to it.

MOM:
Are any of your friends home right now?

SCARLET:
A few of them are. I'll give them a call.

MOM:
It might be good to get out and get your mind off things.

Stalker

SCARLET:
Yeah maybe.

MOM:
Did Brady come down with you?

SCARLET:
No, he had to work to do on campus and they wouldn't give him the time off. He's coming down tomorrow.

MOM:
It'll be nice to finally meet him.

SCARLET:
Kind of a crappy time for it to happen.

MOM:
I know baby.

The phone rings.

MOM:
Hello?
(pause)
Yes, just a second.
(hands the phone to Scarlet)
It's for you.

Scarlet takes the phone.

SCARLET:
Thanks. Hello?
(pause)
Oh, hey Jamie.
(pause)
About as good as a funeral can be.
(pause)
No, it's okay.
(pause)
Yeah, but it's out of your way.
(pause)
Fine, if you insist.
(pause)
Alright, bye.

MOM:
What's going on?

SCARLET:
Oh, Jamie wants to head out shopping then to the club.

MOM:
Kind of early for that isn't it?

SCARLET:
She can take forever in a mall.

MOM:
You gonna be okay doing that?

SCARLET:
Aren't you the one who said I needed to get out?

MOM:
(laughs)
Yes, okay, go have fun.

SCARLET:
Mom?

MOM:
Yeah?

SCARLET:
Thanks.

MOM:
For what?

SCARLET:
Just...everything.

MOM:
Well, you're welcome.

INT. - SHOPPING MALL – DAY

Scarlet and JAMIE, another young female college aged student, are coming out of a lingerie store. Jamie is laughing.

JAMIE:
Oh come on, it would have looked good on you.

SCARLET:
I'm really not in the mood to be buying lingerie right now.

JAMIE:
Brady would love it.

SCARLET:
Well that's true.

JAMIE:
If the sex is as good as you say it is, this could make it even better.

SCARLET:
(laughs)
That's enough.

JOHN walks up behind them.

JOHN:
Sex? Who's having sex.

JAMIE:
Well, Scarlet would be if she'd just listen to me.

SCARLET:
I think I'm going to call off sex if you keep talking about it.

JOHN:
Oh come on, you?

SCARLET:
Me what?

Stalker

JOHN:
Having sex? This is different than the super conservative church girl I dated.

SCARLET:
Well ever since my parents divorced, things have changed.

JOHN:
Obviously.

SCARLET:
You're just jealous.

JOHN:
Ha, I'm happy with what I'm getting now.

JAMIE:
You better be.

JOHN:
It's never been better.

JAMIE:
Good.

SCARLET:
Well this is kind of awkward.

JOHN:
Yeah just a wee-bit.

JAMIE:
Then let's stop talking about it.

SCARLET:
See? Now you know how strange it is picking out someone else's lingerie.

JAMIE:
I could send him in with you.

John looks at Jamie with an eyebrow raised.

SCARLET:
Umm, no thank you. Can we move on please?

JAMIE:
Sure thing.

SCARLET:
Is anyone else joining us tonight?

JAMIE:
Yeah, you remember Jeremy?

SCARLET:
Yeah, he was the quiet and shy one in high school.

JAMIE:
Yeah, that's him.

SCARLET:
How'd you two end up becoming friends?

JAMIE:
We ended up talking a lot when we worked at the factory together one summer.

SCARLET:
He talked?

JAMIE:
It took a bit of coaxing.

SCARLET:
I don't want to know.

JAMIE:
No, not like that.

SCARLET:
(to John)
And you weren't jealous?

JOHN:
Was at first, till I talked to him.

SCARLET:
Then what?

JOHN:
Then I saw he wasn't a threat, guy could barely say two words to me.

SCARLET:
Ah I see.

Scarlet's cellphone rings.

JAMIE:
That your phone?

SCARLET:
Yeah, it's a text message.

JAMIE:
From who?

SCARLET:
(gets giddy)
From Brady, he's gonna be here tonight.

JAMIE:
I thought he wasn't going to be here till tomorrow.

SCARLET:
Hey, I'm not complaining.

Scarlet looks at Jamie.

SCARLET:
I'll be right back.

JAMIE:
Where are you going?

Scarlet goes back into the store.

Stalker

    JAMIE:
     (smiling)
I knew it.

INT. - NIGHT CLUB – NIGHT

    The night club is in a basement in a downtown location. Colored lights are in the ceiling and strobe lights flash with the beat of the bass. A light mist is one the dance floor. LAURA, CYNTHIA and JEREMY are waiting by a bar.

    LAURA:
     (excitedly)
Jamie. Scarlet, I am so sorry girl.

    SCARLET:
Thanks.

    LAURA:
Are you okay?

    SCARLET:
No, but it'll get better with time.

    Laura hugs Scarlet.

    LAURA:
If there's anything I can do for you, just let me know okay?

    SCARLET:
Sure thing.

    CYNTHIA:
Tonight we mourn and celebrate each other, amen?

    EVERYONE:
Amen.

    Jamie and John go off to the dance floor and start dancing. Laura and Cynthia take shots off the bar and down them. Scarlet looks on and smiles. She orders a screwdriver from the bar and takes a drink.

    LAURA:
So tell us about this Brady.

    SCARLET:
You'll meet him tonight.

    LAURA:
Really? He's going to be here?

    SCARLET:
Yup.

    LAURA:
Maybe I'll have to steal him from you.

    SCARLET:
You didn't steal enough of my boyfriends in high school?

    LAURA:
I've apologized for that.

SCARLET:
I know, but you're still a whore.

Laura laughs.

LAURA:
People change.

SCARLET:
Apparently they don't.

LAURA:
Hey, that's harsh.

BRADY emerges from the entrance as a dark shadow. He moves across the room and walks up behind SCARLET. His face can't be seen.

SCARLET:
I didn't mean it.

LAURA:
I know.

Brady reaches out to touch Scarlet. Laura screams and pulls Scarlet away. Scarlet screams with her.

BRADY:
Whoa, sorry, this is my girlfriend.

LAURA:
You're Brady?

BRADY:
Yeah.

Laura and Cynthia both look at Scarlet.

SCARLET:
Yes, this is the love of my life.

BRADY:
I love it when you say that.

Scarlet smiles.

LAURA:
Aww, how sweet.

CYNTHIA:
Please, don't make me sick.

LAURA:
Don't you have a date to suck on?

CYNTHIA:
No, but I got my eyes on someone.

LAURA:
Who?

CYNTHIA:
Her.

Stalker

Cynthia points to AUDREY a girl with long flowing blonde hair in a dark green dress.

SCARLET:
When did you come out of the closet?

CYNTHIA:
Oh, about a year ago.

LAURA:
You think that girl is gay?

CYNTHIA:
If she's not, she soon will be.

Scarlet points at Laura and Cynthia.

SCARLET:
Maybe you two should hook up.

CYNTHIA:
Don't think I haven't thought about it.

Cynthia smiles then makes her way over to Audrey. She talks to her and the two go off to the other end of the bar.

LAURA:
At least she won't be hitting on me tonight.

BRADY:
Interesting friends you have here.

SCARLET:
This is all new to me.

Laura smiles.

SCARLET:
(to Laura)
If I didn't know better, I'd say you like her attention.

LAURA:
(shrugs)
Sometimes.

SCARLET:
(shocked)
Have you ever...you know...with her?

Laura smiles then goes off to the dance floor.

BRADY:
Very interesting friends.

SCARLET:
Yeah, yeah. Just keep your little friend focused on me.

BRADY:
No problem there.

Brady leans in and kisses Scarlet. Scarlet walks over to Jeremy.

SCARLET:
You haven't said a whole lot.

JEREMY:
Sorry, I'm not much of a talker.

SCARLET:
Just like when we were younger?

JEREMY:
Yeah, pretty much.

BRADY:
It's okay man, lighten up.

JEREMY:
Sorry, I'm just a little shy around...

SCARLET:
Around?

JEREMY:
Around women, particularly you.

SCARLET:
What?

BRADY:
What?

JEREMY:
Sorry, I don't mean anything by it. I used to have a huge crush on you. I don't anymore but it still makes me nervous to talk to people, you know remembering that.

BRADY:
Well that's kind of awkward.

Scarlet scowls at Brady.

SCARLET:
You got nothing to be afraid of Jeremy, we're all friends here.

JEREMY:
Yeah, sure, okay.

SCARLET:
(to Brady)
Now come on you, I got plans for you.

Brady smiles and allows Scarlet to lead him to the dance floor. Jeremy follows Scarlet with his eyes then goes back to the bar.

INT. - SCARLET'S BEDROOM – NIGHT

Scarlet and Brady are laying naked on the bed together. They are fast asleep. Scarlet suddenly wakes up and pulls on some clothes. She turns around and finds Stalker looking into the window at her. She screams and Stalker runs away.

BRADY:
What?

Stalker
SCARLET:
There's someone out there.

Brady gets up to look, but Stalker is gone.

SCARLET:
There was someone there.

BRADY:
You sure?

SCARLET:
Yes, I'm sure.

Scarlet drapes herself with a sheet and runs into the living room and grabs the phone.

SCARLET:
(to phone)
Yes, there was someone in my yard peeking in on me.
(pause)
He's not there now, he took off when I saw him.
(pause)
I have no idea who it could be.
(pause)
Yes, I'll be home all night.
(pause)
Yes, I'd like to talk to the police. Thank you.

Scarlet hangs up phone. Brady is in the hallway with a pair of pants on. He looks at her with worry in his eyes.

Act 2

INT. - COFFEE SHOP -- DAY

    Scarlet and Jamie are sitting in a coffee shop together. The shop isn't very busy and there is an employee cleaning tables. Scarlet looks a bit shaken and Jamie is concerned.

    JAMIE:
Are you serious?

    SCARLET:
Yes.

    JAMIE:
Do you know who it was?

    SCARLET:
I have no idea.

    JAMIE:
That's freaky.

    SCARLET:
I know.

    JAMIE:
What did the police say?

    SCARLET:
Not much. They did a patrol of the neighborhood and posted a cop outside my house for the night but they didn't catch anyone.

    JAMIE:
So this freak of nature is still out there?

    SCARLET:
Pretty much.

    JAMIE:
That's just too creepy.

    SCARLET:
You don't have to tell me, I was there.

    JAMIE:
What're you going to do?

    SCARLET:
I don't know. I'm not ready to head back to school yet but Brady is pushing to get out of here.

    JAMIE:
Can't really blame him.

SCARLET:
No, but I'm still not ready to leave.

JAMIE:
Why?

SCARLET:
I want to stick around find out if the cops can catch Sara's killer.

JAMIE:
I'm sure if they catch him they'll call you at the campus.

SCARLET:
I'd rather be at home with my mom.

JAMIE:
Is that safe?

SCARLET:
It's the safest place I can think of right now.

JAMIE:
Why do you say that?

SCARLET:
What if this creep follows me? I'd be at school all by myself and who would be around then?

JAMIE:
What about Brady? I thought you two lived together.

SCARLET:
Well we do, but with his job and different class schedule, he's not always around.

JAMIE:
But your mom works too.

SCARLET:
Not nights though, Brady does.

JAMIE:
If this guy wants you he can get you during the day.

SCARLET:
That thought just freaks me out even more.

JAMIE:
I'm just trying to be realistic.

SCARLET:
Thanks for your concern.

JAMIE:
So how was your night otherwise, I mean with Brady?

SCARLET:
That's for me to know and you not to find out.

JAMIE:
Oh come on, tell me.

SCARLET:
Why? Do you have to live vicariously through other people or something?

JAMIE:
No, but I like to know details.

SCARLET:
Well you're not going to get them.

John suddenly appears at the table.

JOHN:
Not going to get what?

JAMIE:
What are you doing here?

JOHN:
I was just walking by and saw you two, thought I'd come in and see the girl I love.

JAMIE:
Well isn't that sweet.

Jamie and John kiss.

JOHN:
Yeah, Jeremy was outside too.

SCARLET:
He was? Why didn't he come inside?

JOHN:
I don't know. I can only guess though.

JAMIE:
That's not like him.

JOHN:
(to Scarlet)
Maybe he's still in love with you.

SCARLET:
He said he's not.

JOHN:
Yeah, okay.

JAMIE:
Is he still out there?

JOHN:
Maybe.

John turns around to look out the front window to the outdoor patio.

JOHN:
Yeah, he's right there.

JAMIE:
(yells)
Jeremy. Come in.

Jeremy looks up and sees Jamie waving her arm. He gets up finishes his coffee and walks off.

Stalker

JAMIE:
Well that was strange.

SCARLET:
Creepy if you ask me.

JAMIE:
He's probably just nervous, doesn't know what to make of all this.

JOHN:
Let's hope that's all it is.

SCARLET:
What're you suggesting?

JOHN:
I don't know.

JAMIE:
You obviously do.

JOHN:
Just maybe he's a little too attached that's all.

SCARLET:
You think he's stalking me?

JOHN:
If you want to be blunt, then yes.

JAMIE:
Sorry, I can't believe that. He's too nice a guy.

JOHN:
Should I be worried?

JAMIE:
With what?

JOHN:
Maybe he's stalking you.

JAMIE:
I doubt it. He's just shy and doesn't know you or Scarlet very well.

JOHN:
Maybe he knows you too well.

JAMIE:
Please, stop. That's a friend you're talking about.

JOHN:
I'm just saying.

JAMIE:
Well don't.

JOHN:
Fine.

Scarlet's cellphone rings.

JAMIE:
Is that Brady again?

SCARLET:
No, it's the police.
(opens phone)
Hello?
(pause)
Yes, detective, how's it going?
(pause)
Really?
(pause)
What does that mean?
(pause)
Okay, thank you.
(pause)
If anything happens I'll let you know.

Scarlet closes her phone.

JAMIE:
What was that all about?

SCARLET:
A detective that is investigating by sister's case says that he thinks it's the same guy that was stalking my sister. He's going to keep an officer outside my house at night for my safety.

JAMIE:
I think you should get out of here hun.

SCARLET:
He'll just follow me, so no.

JOHN:
Do what you think is best.

SCARLET:
Thank you.

Jamie glares at John.

JOHN:
What?

JAMIE:
Nothing.

JOHN:
(sarcastically)
Okay.

JAMIE:
Where is Brady anyway?

SCARLET:
He was tired from the late night drive.

JAMIE:
(laughs)
Oh, I'm sure he was.

Stalker

SCARLET:
Yeah okay, anyway he's at home.

JAMIE:
So what are you going to do now?

SCARLET:
I'm gonna head back home, meet up with him.

JAMIE:
You gonna be alright?

SCARLET:
Yeah, I think so.

JAMIE:
Okay hun, see you tonight.

SCARLET:
Sure thing.

Scarlet gets up and heads for the set of double doors that lead outside.

EXT. - FRONT OF COFFEE SHOP – DAY

Scarlet gets to her car and looks around. Seeing no one she gets in her car and drives off.

INT. - CAR – DAY

Driving down a busy sidewalk Scarlet sees Jeremy and quickly pulls over.

EXT. - SIDEWALK – DAY

Scarlet gets out of the car.

SCARLET:
Hey.

Jeremy keeps walking.

SCARLET:
Hey, Jeremy.

Jeremy looks behind him and stops.

JEREMY:
Oh, hey Scarlet.

SCARLET:
What's going on?

JEREMY:
N...nothing.

SCARLET:
Were you outside my house last night?

JEREMAY:
What? N...no.

SCARLET:
Getting your rocks off watching me?

JEREMY:
No, I swear I was nowhere near your place.

SCARLET:
I don't believe you.

JEREMY:
I wouldn't do that to you.

SCARLET:
Whatever, don't come around my place again. The cops will be there.

JEREMY:
It wasn't me.

SCARLET:
Just stay away.

Scarlet gets back in her car and drives off. A car pulls out of a parking spot and follows her down the road.

EXT. - OUTSIDE MOM'S HOUSE – DAY

Scarlet pulls the car into the drive way. The car that was following her drives past. It slows down and drives off. As Scarlet gets out of the car she sees the car drive off and shakes her head. She walks to the front door and goes in.

INT. - MOM'S HOUSE – DAY

Scarlet walks into the front door and sets her purse down on a side table.

MOM:
Scarlet, baby, is that you?

SCARLET:
Yes mom, I'm home.

MOM:
Where'd you go?

SCARLET:
To have some coffee with Jamie.

MOM:
Well that's nice. I haven't seen her in awhile. How's she doing?

SCARLET:
Good, she's dating John, my ex.

MOM:
Ah, I see.
(pause)
I didn't hear you come in last night.

SCARLET:
We came back late. Did you get my note?

MOM:
Yes, it was a weird way to meet Brady though.

SCARLET:
Sorry.

MOM:
I could hear you two last night.

SCARLET:
What can I say? He's good.

MOM:
You know I don't approve.

SCARLET:
I'm a big girl, I can make my own decisions.

MOM:
I know, but I still feel that I have to say something.

SCARLET:
Well don't.
(pause)
Where's Brady?

MOM:
He went to the superstore, there were some things he forgot and needed to pick up.

SCARLET:
Okay. When did he leave?

MOM:
About a half hour ago, said he wouldn't be long.

SCARLET:
That's good.

MOM:
You never told me how you two met.

SCARLET:
We sat beside each other in a sociology class. He asked me out one day and the rest is history.

MOM:
I see.

SCARLET:
What?

MOM:
It was just strange waking up and there's a strange man in my house.

SCARLET:
He's harmless.

MOM:
After what happened to your sister, I have reason to be concerned.

SCARLET:
Okay, I'm sorry.

MOM:
Just be more careful please.

SCARLET:
Yes, okay I will.

Mom turns around grabs a towel and starts drying some dishes.

MOM:
Any plans for tonight?

SCARLET:
Yeah, I'm going to see a movie with the girls tonight.

MOM:
Is Brady going with you?

SCARLET:
Of course.

MOM:
What movie?

SCARLET:
That new horror movie that's out.

MOM:
You still watching those?

SCARLET:
Some things don't change.

MOM:
Apparently others do.

SCARLET:
Mom, don't start on that again.

MOM:
I'm sorry, I won't say anything else.

SCARLET:
Thank you.

Brady walks in the front door.

SCARLET:
Hey babe.

BRADY:
Hey.

SCARLET:
Pick up what you need?

BRADY:
Yeah, your mom tell you what I had to do?

SCARLET:
Yeah she did.

BRADY:
Yeah, smart.

SCARLET:
It's okay, don't be hard on yourself.

MOM:
So what did you two want to do for supper? Or are you heading out before then?

SCARLET:
We're going to the late show, so we'll be around.

MOM:
Good.

INT. - CYNTHIA'S APARTMENT – NIGHT

Cynthia and Audrey are making out on the couch in a very well decorated apartment. Cynthia moans in pleasure as Audrey kisses her neck. She looks over at the clock and sees that it is 9 pm.

CYNTHIA:
We're going to be late.

AUDREY:
Late for what?

CYNTHIA:
The movie I told you about.

AUDREY:
So?

CYNTHIA:
I'd like you to meet my friends.

AUDREY:
We haven't even been together a full day yet, let's take it a little slower.

CYNTHIA:
Whatever you want, but I still need to be going.

AUDREY:
Oh come on, stay a little longer.

CYNTHIA:
I can't, I promised I'd go.

AUDREY:
One more orgasm, come on.

CYNTHIA:
You're twisting my rubber arm.

AUDREY:
Is it working?

CYNTHIA:
If I didn't promise I'd go tonight, I'd be back on top of you. But a promise is a promise.

AUDREY:
Okay if you say so.

Cynthia and Audrey kiss once more. Audrey picks up her purse then heads out of the apartment. Cynthia walks up to a mirror fixes her make-up and straightens her clothes before heading out.

EXT. - DARK STREET – NIGHT

Cynthia walks out, locks her door then starts walking down the street. Her heels echo as she walks down the sidewalk. Stalker's shadow appears behind her and starts following her. Cynthia turns around and the shadow disappears.

CYNTHIA:
Hello?

Silence.

CYNTHIA:
I must be crazy.

Cynthia's cellphone rings.

CYNTHIA:
Hello?
(pause)
Yeah I know, I'm on my way now.
(pause)
Okay Jamie, just wait a few minutes, I'll be there soon.
(pause)
Okay, bye.

Cynthia hangs up her cellphone. As she's walking she starts humming a tune. She turns around just as the rustling from a bush is heard.

CYNTHIA:
Hello? Audrey is that you?

Silence.

CYNTHIA:
This is starting to get ridiculous. You're freaking me out.

Silence.

CYNTHIA:
I'll call you when I get home, okay?

Silence.

CYNTHIA:
(mumbling)
I thought she'd be different, oh well.

She starts humming again. Cynthia comes to a break in the tune and a male voice is heard finishing the tune.

CYNTHIA:
Okay, who's there?

Stalker comes out of the bushes.

CYNTHIA:
Who are you?

STALKER:
That doesn't matter.

Stalker

CYNTHIA:
I think it does.

STALKER:
You'll find out soon enough.

CYNTHIA:
You should know, I don't swing for men.

STALKER:
You shouldn't have changed.

CYNTHIA:
Excuse me?

STALKER:
You shouldn't have changed.

CYNTHIA:
I can't help it, I was made this way.

STALKER:
No, you're deranged, and I'm going to set things right.

CYNTHIA:
Please just leave me alone.

STALKER:
I can't do that.

Cynthia starts running. Stalker walks after her. Cynthia looks behind her panicked and trips on her heels.

CYNTHIA:
Please, I didn't do anything.

STALKER:
Yes, you did.

CYNTHIA:
What becoming gay?

STALKER:
Yes, you changed.

CYNTHIA:
So what.

STALKER:
And you will be the beginning to my purge.

CYNTHIA:
Please I'll do anything. Just leave me alone.

STALKER:
You've already done it.

Stalker kneels beside her and plunges a knife into her chest. She screams but he covers her mouth with his hand. He then slits her throat. Blood pools on the sidewalk and Stalker leaves.

INT. - THEATER LOBBY – NIGHT

> *Jamie, Laura, Scarlet and Brady are waiting in the lobby and getting visibly frustrated. Jamie checks her cellphone then rolls her eyes.*

LAURA:
Where is she?

JAMIE:
I don't know, I'll try calling her again.

> *Jamie hits a button on her cellphone and holds it up to her ear. She waits a few moments then puts the phone back in her purse.*

JAMIE:
No answer.

SCARLET:
How about John? Isn't he coming?

JAMIE:
No, he had to work tonight.

SCARLET:
That's too bad.

JAMIE:
Him working pays for me tonight.

BRADY:
Must be nice.

JAMIE:
Oh it is.

BRADY:
What about that Jeremy?

JAMIE:
Well you kind of traumatized him, Scarlet.

SCARLET:
He was acting weird and I didn't like it.

JAMIE:
Yes well, trying being a little more sensitive.

> *Scarlet and Brady roll their eyes.*

LAURA:
I'm getting worried.

JAMIE:
She shouldn't be much longer.

LAURA:
Cynthia is always fashionably late, but never this late.

JAMIE:
I know. The movie is starting, we can't wait anymore.

Stalker

LAURA:
Alright, let's go sit down then.

INT. - THEATER LOBBY – NIGHT

The group emerges from the theater. They all put a drink in the garbage.

SCARLET:
Well that was lame.

JAMIE:
It wasn't that bad.

LAURA:
Yeah, yeah it was.

JAMIE:
C'mon we've seen worse.

LAURA:
I just wish Cynthia was here. She would have said something about it.

JAMIE:
Yes well, it's too late now.

Audrey walks up to them and they all look at her strangely.

JAMIE:
Can we help you?

AUDREY:
It's Cynthia.

LAURA:
Oh, you're that girl from the club.

AUDREY:
Yeah, Audrey.

LAURA:
What about Cynthia?

AUDREY:
(crying)
She's dead.

JAMIE:
What?

AUDREY:
She was stabbed.

SCARLET:
When?

AUDREY:
I don't know. I left her place so she could come here. I came back a few hours later though because I wanted to surprise her and I came across her thrown into a bush. I called the police and they're all there now.

SCARLET:
Who did it?

AUDREY:
They don't know.

LAURA:
I want to go see.

SCARLET:
They probably got it all taped off. We won't even get close.

LAURA:
I don't care.

JAMIE:
We can always call the police.

LAURA:
No, she was special to me, I want to see her.

JAMIE:
Okay, let's go. I'll call John on the way.

EXT. - DARK STREET – NIGHT

The street is filled with police cruisers and news vans. The girls walk up to the yellow tape and try to see over the press. FRIENDLY DETECTIVE and COCKY REPORTER and talking.

FRIENDLY DETECTIVE:
The body has been identified and we are informing the family right now.

COCKY REPORTER:
Is there any connection to the murder last week?

FRIENDLY DETECTIVE:
It's too early to draw any conclusions but so far there are similarities that are being investigated.

COCKY REPORTER:
What kind of similarities?

FRIENDLY DETECTIVE:
That's all I'm saying for now.

The reporter snorts angrily then walks off with the camera man. The group of girls walk up to the yellow tape.

SCARLET:
Detective?

FRIENDLY DETECTIVE:
Yes?
(turns around)
Scarlet? What are you doing here?

SCARLET:
Is it Cynthia?

FRIENDLY DETECTIVE:
Yes, I'm afraid it is. You shouldn't be here.

SCARLET:
Why?

FRIENDLY DETECTIVE:
It's pretty brutal. She was killed similarly to your sister. We think it's the same guy.

LAURA:
Why haven't you done anything?

FRIENDLY DETECTIVE:
We're trying, but none of the neighbors say they saw anything.

LAURA:
How is that possible? It was right in front of their homes.

FRIENDLY DETECTIVE:
I know how it looks, but honestly we're doing our best.

LAURA:
Well it's not enough.

Laura starts crying

SCARLET:
Do you think there's any other connection to the deaths?

FRIENDLY DETECTIVE:
We have our theories but I'm not going to comment on them right now.

SCARLET:
It would help if you would.

FRIENDLY DETECTIVE:
I'm sorry but I can't.

John comes running up.

JOHN:
Can I see her?

FRIENDLY DETECTIVE:
I'm sorry but we can't allow anyone into the crime scene.

JOHN:
She was a friend of mine.

FRIENDLY DETECTIVE:
I'm sorry, but we can't allow it.

Jamie hugs John and starts crying. Scarlet and Brady walk off.

BRADY:
What're you thinking?

SCARLET:
It's just weird that my sister and now a friend of mine is the one dying.

BRADY:
You think there's some kind of connection to you?

SCARLET:
I hope not.

BRADY:
Let's not jump to conclusions okay. We'll know more once the police do their jobs.

SCARLET:
Yeah, you're right. I'm just scared.

BRADY:
We all are.

SCARLET:
Detective?

FRIENDLY DETECTIVE:
Yes?

SCARLET:
Our friend, Jeremy, has been acting strange lately. Maybe you should try talking to him.

JAMIE:
(screaming)
Scarlet.

SCARLET:
Sorry, but I don't trust him.

JAMIE:
That was uncalled for.

FRIENDLY DETECTIVE:
Thanks Scarlet, we'll look into it.

Act 3

INT. - MOM'S LIVING ROOM – DAY

> *Scarlet is sitting on the couch crying. Brady is there trying to console her.*

BRADY:
It'll be okay.

SCARLET:
How can you say that?

BRADY:
I don't know.

SCARLET:
It's not your family and friends who are dying.

BRADY:
It could just be coincidence.

SCARLET:
I don't believe it is.

BRADY:
They'll get that Jeremy guy, I'm sure of it.

SCARLET:
They better.

BRADY:
Why don't we do something to cheer you up?

SCARLET:
I'm not interested.

BRADY:
Doing something is better than sitting here crying.

SCARLET:
Can't you let me mourn my friends?

BRADY:
Sorry.

SCARLET:
It wouldn't hurt to be a little more sensitive.

BRADY:
Again, I'm sorry. We've been here for awhile and I'm getting agitated.

SCARLET:
Fine, what do you want to do?

BRADY:
Want to watch a movie?

SCARLET:
Sure.

BRADY:
That sounded convincing.

SCARLET:
This is your idea, not mine.

Scarlet wipes a tear away from her face.

BRADY:
Alright, how about a comedy? Something to lighten the mood.

SCARLET:
Whatever.

Brady goes to a shelf with movies on it and picks one out. He walks over to the TV And puts the DVD in.

BRADY:
I do wish there was something I could do to make you feel better.

SCARLET:
I know.

BRADY:
Is there anything I can do?

SCARLET:
I don't know. I'm still trying to piece everything together.

BRADY:
Alright.

Brady sits down next to Scarlet when a knock is heard on the door.

BRADY:
Who could that be?

SCARLET:
I don't know.

Scarlet goes and answers the front door. Friendly Detective is there waiting.

SCARLET:
Detective, what can I do for you?

FRIENDLY DETECTIVE:
Just wanted to go over a few details with you.

SCARLET:
Sure anything I can help with.

FRIENDLY DETECTIVE:
Where were you the night of your sisters death?

SCARLET:
Excuse me?

FRIENDLY DETECTIVE:
Please answer the question.

SCARLET:
In my campus apartment doing homework. What does this have to do with Jeremy?

FRIENDLY DETECTIVE:
Do you have anyone that can testify to that?

SCARLET:
Am I a suspect?

FRIENLY DETECTIVE:
I'm not saying you are, but my captain wanted me to question you. If you have an alibi then you can be taken off the list right away.

SCARLET:
This is bullshit.

FRIENDLY DETECTIVE:
So you don't have one?

SCARLET:
Yes, I do. You can call one of my roommates, they'll tell you I was there.

FRIENDLY DETECTIVE:
Do you have the number?

Scarlet grabs a piece of paper and scribbles a number down on it.

FRIENDLY DETECTIVE:
Thank you.

SCARLET:
What about Jeremy? Did you talk to him yet?

FRIENDLY DETECTIVE:
Yes we have.

SCARLET:
And?

FRIENDLY DETECTIVE:
He has a rock solid alibi.

SCARLET:
What?

FRIENDLY DETECIVE:
His whole family can confirm that he was home with his parents the night of Cynthia's death.

SCARLET:
I'm sure it's him though.

FRIENDLY DETECTIVE:
I'm afraid to tell you that you're wrong.

SCARLET:
Besides me, are there any other leads?

FRIENDLY DETECTIVE:
I can't really say.

SCARLET:
(frustrated)
Oh come on.

FRIEDNLY DETECTIVE:
Okay, we're coming up dry but we're investigating everything we come across.

SCARLET:
There's my tax dollars at work.

FRIENDLY DETECTIVE:
We're trying our best.

SCARLET:
Is there anything else detective?

FRIENDLY DETECTIVE:
No, that is all. Just let us know if you plan on leaving town at all.

Mom comes running into the house.

MOM:
Is everything okay?

FRIENDLY DETECTIVE:
Yes, everything's fine. I was just leaving.

MOM:
What's going on?

Friendly Detective walks off.

SCARLET:
He was asking me questions.

MOM:
For what?

SCARLET:
They think I may have done it.

MOM:
(angrily)
What?

SCARLET:
That's what I said.

MOM:
You weren't even around.

SCARLET:
I know.

BRADY:
So I guess we're not heading back to campus anytime soon.

SCARLET:
No, it doesn't look like it.

Stalker's dark shadow is seen looking through the front door with a pair of binoculars from across the street. The door closes and he vanishes.

BRADY:
So now what?

SCARLET:
Now we wait till the next death.

INT. - COFFEE HOUSE – DAY

Jamie is sitting at a table. She is showing signs of impatience as she waits for someone to show up. She checks her cellphone and rolls her eyes. After a few moments Jeremy shows up.

JEREMY:
Mind if I sit down?

JAMIE:
Took you long enough to get here.

JEREMY:
Sorry, had some errands to do.

JAMIE:
Yes, sit please.

JEREMY:
Thank you.

Jeremy sits down across from Jamie.

JAMIE:
What are you doing?

JEREMY:
What're you talking about?

JAMIE;
Are you the one killing people?

JEREMY:
If I was do you think I'd tell you?

JAMIE:
That's kind of freaky.

JEREMY:
No it's not me.

JAMIE:
Cops were at my door asking me for an alibi and asking questions about you.

JEREMY:
Yeah they showed up at my door late last night.

JAMIE:
That didn't take them long.

JEREMY:
What do you mean?

JAMIE:
Scarlet spilled your name to the police.

JEREMY:
What? Why would she do that?

JAMIE:
Let's just say she isn't exactly a fan of yours.

JEREMY:
I can tell.

JAMIE:
And frankly you've been acting weird ever since she came back into town.

JEREMY:
Yeah, sorry.

JAMIE:
So what is going on?

JEREMY:
I dunno, I'm just nervous.

JAMIE:
Do you still have feelings for her?

JEREMY:
Not really.

JAMIE:
Not really?

JEREMY:
Okay, yes I do.

JAMIE:
You better get yourself under control then.

JEREMY:
It's hard seeing her again.

JAMIE:
Well you better start acting like your life depends on it.

JEREMY:
You don't think this creep will come after me?

JAMIE:
I don't know.

JEREMY:
I'm getting kind of scared.

JAMIE:
We all are.

JEREMY:
What are you going to do?

JAMIE:
I'm going to wait a few day then head out of town.

JEREMY:
The police told me not to leave town.

JAMIE:
Same here, but I don't plan on listening.

JEREMY:
That will put you high on their suspect list.

JAMIE:
I don't care. It's either that or die.

JEREMY:
Good point.

JAMIE:
What are you going to do?

JEREMY:
Maybe I should go talk to Scarlet.

JAMIE:
I wouldn't suggest that.

JEREMY:
Why not?

JAMIE:
For one, there's a cop outside her place 24/7. Second she's not exactly all that fond of you right now.

JEREMY:
But it wasn't me. If I go and explain that to her.

JAMIE:
I don't think it'll help. I'd just lie low and wait for this to blow over.

JEREMY:
Alright, if you think that's best.

JAMIE:
I don't know what's best. That's why I can't wait to get out of here.

JEREMY:
Well, good luck. Wherever you're going.

JAMIE:
Thanks you too.

Jamie gets up and leaves. Jeremy pulls out a cellphone and starts texting.

INT. - MOM'S LIVING ROOM – DAY

Brady and Scarlet are sitting on the couch watching a movie. Brady is laughing quietly while Scarlet just stares at the screen not showing any emotion.

BRADY:
Come on, at least try and enjoy the movie.

SCARLET:
I told you I didn't want to do this.

BRADY:
What do you want to do then?

SCARLET:
I don't know.

Scarlet's cellphone rings.

BRADY:
What is that?

Scarlet pulls out her cellphone and looks at it.

SCARLET:
It's a text message.

BRADY:
From who?

SCARLET:
I don't know. I don't recognize the number.

BRADY:
What does it say?

Scarlet gasps and covers her mouth.

BRADY:
What does it say?

SCARLET:
It's says 'I'm watching you.'

BRADY:
How'd he get your cellphone number?

SCARLET:
I don't know.

INSERT – SCREEN OF CELLPHONE

A text types on the screen "Leave me alone." The text gets sent. A second later another text comes in. "You will be mine. I will have you."

BACK TO LIVING ROOM

BRADY:
This Jeremy is starting to freak me out.

INSERT – SCREEN OF CELLPHONE

Scarlet types "Just leave me alone Jeremy." A second later another text comes. "I will not. I've waited to long for this."

BACK TO LIVING ROOM

BRADY:
Maybe you should go tell that cop across the street.

SCARLET:
That's a good idea.

Scarlet heads to the front door and goes outside.

EXT. - IN FRONT OF MOM'S HOUSE – DAY

    Scarlet walks up to the cop cruiser across the street. BORED COP is sitting there writing in his notebook. He doesn't notice Scarlet walk up to him.

    SCARLET:
Excuse me?

    BORED COP:
Yes? Can I help you?

    SCARLET:
This creep we're looking for just texted me.

    BORED COP:
Let's see.

    Scarlet give him her cellphone and he checks the messages.

    BORED COP:
I'll let the detective know immediately. I'm going to copy down this number. Hopefully we can track it to whoever it's registered to.

    SCARLET:
Let's hope so.

    BORED COP:
Hopefully this is his crucial mistake.

    Bored Cop picks up his cellphone and makes a call. Scarlet walks off back to the house.

INT. - MOM'S LIVING ROOM – DAY

    BRADY:
What did the cop say?

    SCARLET:
He took some notes and is calling the detective.

    BRADY:
That's good.

    SCARLET:
Hopefully they can catch him.

    A knock is heard at the door. Scarlet opens the door and it is the Bored Cop.

    SCARLET:
Get anything?

    BORED COP:
Unfortunately no.

    SCARLET:
What?

    BORED COP:
The cellphone was a disposable one.

    SCARLET:
I don't understand.

BORED COP:
It was one of those cheap phones you can buy in a variety store.

SCARLET:
Great.

BORED COP:
I thought for sure we'd have something.

SCARLET:
So did I.

BORED COP:
Just hand tight, whoever it is, we'll catch him.

SCARLET:
The quicker the better.

Scarlet's cellphone rings again.

INSERT – CELLPHONE SCREEN

"Bad girl telling the cops, you'll pay for that."

BACK TO LIVING ROOM

SCARLET:
Please let this end.

INT. - JAMIE'S APARTMENT – NIGHT

Jamie is frantically packing. A suitcase is on her bed and she is quickly shoving clothes in it trying to get out of the apartment. John is sitting on the bed next to the suitcase.

JOHN:
Are you sure you should be doing this?

JAMIE:
I'm not just going to wait around for this guy to come for me.

JOHN:
There's no saying he will.

JAMIE:
How do you know that?

JOHN:
Just speculating.

JAMIE:
Yes well, I'm not going to risk my life on speculation.

Anger crosses John's face.

JOHN:
And what about me?

JAMIE:
You're a big boy, you can handle yourself.

JOHN:
So if he does come after you and can't find you, who do you think he's going to come for?

JAMIE:
Sorry, but I'm looking out for me right now.

JOHN:
You could at least offer to take me with you.

JAMIE:
You already said you didn't want to go.

JOHN:
You're right, I don't.

JAMIE:
Then why are you upset about it?

JOHN:
You never even asked.

JAMIE:
I don't have time for this.

JOHN:
This is typical.

JAMIE:
What is?

JOHN:
You running away.

JAMIE:
Excuse me?

JOHN:
You do this all the time.

JAMIE:
I do not.

JOHN:
Yes you do. Whenever something happens that you don't want to deal with you run off.

JAMIE:
It's better than waiting around for something to happen.

JOHN:
What about your job?

JAMIE:
I'll call in sick.

JOHN:
What if this takes awhile to end?

JAMIE:
I'll find a new job.

JOHN:
Just like that?

JAMIE:
I've done it before.

JOHN:
You going to your mom's again?

JAMIE:
I'll stay there for a bit, then move on.

JOHN:
To where?

JAMIE:
I don't know.

JOHN:
Can you at least call me when you get there so we can talk more about this?

JAMIE:
There's not much to talk about, I've already told you what's going on.

JOHN:
Are you ever going to come back?

JAMIE:
One day, when they catch the bastard.

JOHN:
That could be a long time.

JAMIE:
Then better get all the me time you can right now.

JOHN:
So you'll just leave me behind.

JAMIE:
You make it sound so harsh.

JOHN:
It's what you're doing.

JAMIE:
Okay fine. If I get settled somewhere else, you can come out and join me and we can start a new life together somewhere else. That sound better?

JOHN:
I'd rather it be here.

JAMIE:
Not an option right now.

JOHN:
Fine, just go.

JAMIE:
I'm sorry.

JOHN:
Yeah well, I'm not.

John leaves. The sound of the apartment door slamming is heard. Jamie shoves one last shirt in the suitcase then zippers it shut.

INT. - PARKING GARAGE – NIGHT

    Jamie walks into the parking garage and pulls out her keys. She is about to open the trunk when a shadow is seen. Jamie screams and Laura walks up to her.

LAURA:
Where are you going?

JAMIE:
To my mom's.

LAURA:
Ah, I see.

JAMIE:
You're not mad?

LAURA:
No, can't say I blame you.

JAMIE:
John's pretty mad.

LAURA:
Yeah I can imagine.

JAMIE:
What are you going to do?

LAURA:
I'm going to wait around for Cynthia's funeral then get out of here myself.

JAMIE:
What if this is over by then?

LAURA:
What do you mean?

JAMIE:
What if this guy, whoever he is, strikes before then?

LAURA:
It's a risk I'll take. I have to say my final goodbyes.

JAMIE:
You really cared for her didn't you?

LAURA:
I loved her.

JAMIE:
Seriously?

LAURA:
In my own way, yes.

JAMIE:
Did she know?

LAURA:
I don't know. If she did it wasn't because I told her.

JAMIE:
I'm so sorry. How did you know I was leaving?

LAURA:
Jeremy told me.

JAMIE:
Looks like no one can keep a secret anymore.

LAURA:
I was hoping to convince you to stay.

JAMIE:
Not happening.

LAURA:
Please? You're the last real friend I have.

JAMIE:
Scarlet's still here.

LAURA:
I was never really close with her.

JAMIE:
I'm sorry, but I can't stick around.

LAURA:
Yeah, that's what I figured.

JAMIE:
You'll get through this.

LAURA:
Let's hope so.

Jamie gets in her car and drives off.

INT. - JAMIE'S CAR – NIGHT

Jamie's driving. City lights can be seen as she passes them and music is playing from the CD player. She looks a little tense and is constantly checking over her shoulder. When she get into the country she pulls out her cellphone.

JAMIE:
Hi mom, it's me.
(pause)
No, everything is not fine.
(pause)
I'll explain more when I get there, but let's just say it isn't good.
(pause)
I'm scared.
(pause)
I'm on my way now.
(pause)
I'll worry about John later.
(pause)
Okay, I'll see you in a few hours.
(pause)
Yeah, love you too.

Stalker

     Jamie ends the conversation and puts her cellphone back into the center console. She rests her elbow on the window and puts her head in her hand. She sighs as she drives off. Suddenly she is hit from behind.

     JAMIE:
What the hell?

     She is hit again.

     JAMIE:
What the fuck is going on?

     The car that hit her pulls up beside her and Stalker waves for her to pull over.

     JAMIE:
I don't think so.

     Stalker's car pulls to the side and sideswipes Jamie. Jamie holds on for dear life.

     JAMIE:
I can't believe this is happening to me.

     Jamie picks up her cellphone.

     JAMIE:
C'mon pick up.

     She is hit again.

     JAMIE:
John?
     (pause)
It's me.
     (pause)
I'm on the highway, he's here chasing me.
     (pause)
Right now he's hitting me with his car.
     (pause)
I don't know what to do.
     (pause)
Okay, I'll keep driving.
     (pause)
You'll call the police? Thank you.

     Jamie's car is hit again and she losses control. Her car slides into the ditch and flips over. After the car is done rolling a couple of times, Jamie manages to crawl out of the mess. She gets up and sees Stalker standing on the side of the road.

     JAMIE:
     (yelling)
Please don't.

     Stalker moves towards Jamie.

     JAMIE:
I didn't do anything.

     STALKER:
Are you sure about that?

     JAMIE:
Yes, I'm sure.

STALKER:
Then what are you doing out here?

JAMIE:
What are you talking about?

STALKER:
You left.

JAMIE:
I'm just trying to save myself.

Jamie trips over a rock as she tries to walks backwards.

STALKER:
Foolish girl. You really think you could have avoided me?

JAMIE:
I had to try.

STALKER:
Now you will pay for your sins.

Stalker starts to stab Jamie. Blood flies through the air and Jamie screams into the night. Blood soaks the ground and Jamie dies as she takes her last breath.

INT. - SCARLET'S BEDROOM – NIGHT

Scarlet and Brady are laying in bed trying to get some sleep. Scarlet is wide awake but Brady is out cold. Her cellphone rings and Scarlet jumps. Brady wakes up with the ringing.

BRADY:
Who is it now?

SCARLET:
It's from that same number as before.

BRADY:
What does Jeremy want now?

Scarlet hit a button on her phone and gasps.

INSERT – CELLPHONE SCREEN

A picture of Jamie's dead face appears on the screen with a message "This is what I'm going to do to you."

BACK TO BEDROOM

SCARLET:
Shit.

BRADY:
What?

Scarlet shows Brady the cellphone.

BRADY:
You should call the police right now.

Scarlet pulls on some clothes then runs out to the phone. She dials a number and waits.

Stalker

SCARLET:
Yes, hello? Is this the detective?
(pause)
It's Scarlet. I think something has happened.
(pause)
I just got a text message on my phone. It was a picture of my friend Jamie. It looks like she's dead.
(pause)
I don't know.
(pause)
Okay I'll wait for you to get here.

Scarlet hangs up the phone.

BRADY:
What did he say?

SCARLET:
He's on his way here to look at the picture.

MOM:
What's going on?

SCARLET:
It's Jamie, I think she's dead.

MOM:
What? I'm so sorry.

Scarlet begins to cry. Mom walks over and hugs her.

MOM:
What can I do?

SCARLET:
I don't know.

Act 4

EXT. - MOM'S HOUSE – NIGHT

    Two more police cars are at Mom's house. The Friendly Detective gets out of one of the cars, walks up to the front door and knocks. After a couple of knocks Mom answers the door.

MOM:
Detective. What can I do for you?

FRIENDLY DETECTIVE:
We would like to talk to Scarlet if that's possible.

MOM:
Sure she's in the living room.

INT. - MOM'S LIVING ROOM – NIGHT

    Friendly Detective and two officers walk into the living room. Brady and Scarlet are sitting on the couch. Brady is trying to console the crying Scarlet.

SCARLET:
I'm going to die, aren't I?

FRIENDLY DETECTIVE:
I'm gonna do everything to keep that from happening.

SCARLET:
Why couldn't you protect my friends?

FRIENDLY DETECTIVE:
We're going to start.

SCARLET:
It's a little late.

FRIENDLY DETECTIVE:
Not for Laura it's not.

SCARLET:
She's not going to want a cop sitting out front of her apartment.

FRIENDLY DETECTIVE:
It'll be the best thing for her right now.

SCARLET:
Is there anything else we can do?

FRIENLY DETECTIVE:
Not at the moment.

SCARLET:
Have you found Jamie?

FRIENDLY DETECTIVE:
Not yet. There aren't any clues to where she is in those pictures.

SCARLET:
(crying)
So we won't even be able to say goodbye.

FRIENDLY DETECTIVE:
We'll find her and get this guy.

SCARLET:
I have a hard time believing you.

FRIENDLY DETECTIVE:
I won't rest until this is solved.

SCARLET:
Alright, fine.
(pause)
Am I still a suspect?

FRIENDLY DETECTIVE:
It's safe to say you're not.

SCARLET:
Well that's a relief.

FRIENDLY DETECTIVE:
Is there anyone else you can think of that might be doing this?

SCARLET:
I don't know. I still think it's Jeremy.

FRIENDLY DETECTIVE:
We're certain that it's not him.

Scarlet sighs.

SCARLET:
Then I got nothing for you.

FRIENDLY DETECTIVE:
Alright, we'll be in touch.

SCARLET:
Please whatever you have to do to end this, just do it.

FRIENDLY DETECIVE:
We will, I promise.

Friendly Detective and the two cops leave. Mom closes the door after then and sits in a chair across from Scarlet.

MOM:
What do you want to do?

SCARLET:
I'm starting to think I need to get out of here.

MOM:
I think that would be best.

BRADY:
Are you sure it's safe to leave?

MOM:
What do you mean?

BRADY:
Well cause he followed Jamie didn't he?

SCARLET:
What are you suggesting?

BRADY:
At least here we have police protection.

SCARLET:
We're also in the most danger here.

BRADY:
I think we'll be in more danger at the campus.

SCARLET:
Alright, if you think here is best.

BRADY:
I honestly do.

MOM:
You have a point.

SCARLET:
(crying)
I just want this to end.

MOM:
We all do. Maybe you should try and get some more sleep.

SCARLET:
I'm not going to be able to sleep.

MOM:
At least try.

SCARLET:
Sure.

INT. - MOM'S KITCHEN – DAY

Mom is up cooking when Scarlet walks into the kitchen in her bed clothes. Mom walks up and hugs her.

MOM:
How are you doing?

SCARLET:
Not good.

MOM:
Maybe you should go see a doctor, see if they can give you anything to help you relax.

SCARLET:
Might not be a bad idea.

Stalker
     The phone rings. Mom walks up and answers it.

     MOM:
Hello?
     (pause)
Yes, just a second. Scarlet it's your father.

     Scarlet takes the phone.

     SCARLET:
Hello?
     (pause)
Are you serious?
     (pause)
Yeah, I'd like that.
     (pause)
Alright, bye.

     Scarlet hangs up the phone. Brady comes in the room.

     MOM:
What's going on?

     SCARLET:
The police have opened up dad's house again.

     MOM:
Are you going over there?

     SCARLET:
Yeah, I want to see where Sara died.

     MOM:
Okay, just be careful out there.

     SCARLET:
Sure, mom.

     BRADY:
Did you want me to come with?

     SCARLET:
No, I would rather do this by myself.

     BRADY:
I'm kind of concerned about your safety.

     SCARLET:
I'll be fine.

     BRADY:
Okay.

     Scarlet heads back to the bedroom.

INT. - DAD'S LIVING ROOM – DAY

     Dad is sitting on a chair watching T.V. The house is a little run down but is liveable. A knocking is heard at the door. Dad gets up to answer it and Scarlet is there waiting.

     DAD:
Hey honey.

SCARLET:
Hey Dad.

DAD:
How're you holding up?

SCARLET:
Not well.

DAD:
Did you come from your mom's?

SCARLET:
No, I went to the doctor.

DAD:
For what?

SCARLET:
Something to help me relax.

DAD:
Did he give you something?

SCARLET:
Yeah, should help me sleep.

DAD:
That's good. I'm worried about you.

SCARLET:
Everybody is.

DAD:
Well, come in.

Scarlet walks in.

SCARLET:
Where did it happen?

DAD:
In the bathroom

Scarlet walks down the back hallway to a bathroom. There is still some stains on the floor from the blood.

SCARLET:
They could have cleaned it up when they left.

DAD:
It was worse when I came back in here.

SCARLET:
I wouldn't have been able to handle that.

DAD:
How do you think I felt?

Scarlet leans down and strokes the blood stained tiles.

Stalker
     SCARLET:
     (crying)
Oh, Sara.

     Dad leans down and hugs her.

EXT. - STREET IN FRONT OF COFFEE SHOP – DAY

     *Scarlet's car pulls up into a parking space and Scarlet gets out. She walks up to the coffee shop.
As she does so another car pulls up behind hers. Stalker gets out of the car and sits down on a bench
across from the coffee shop.*

INT. - COFFEE SHOP – DAY

     *Scarlet takes a quick look around when she walks in. She sees Laura and goes and sits down.
Laura does not look happy.*

     LAURA:
Hey.

     SCARLET:
Hey.

     LAURA:
Where were you when I called?

     SCARLET:
I was at my dad's.

     LAURA:
Yeah, I heard the cops were allowing people back in there.

     SCARLET:
Yeah it was rough.
     (pause)
What's wrong? You don't seem like yourself.

     LAURA:
How should I be?

     SCARLET:
What do you mean?

     LAURA:
My friends are all dying around me. You seem to be the only link in this chaos. So I'm sure I'm next.

     SCARLET:
That's not necessarily true.

     LAURA:
Then why is there a cop outside my apartment around the clock?

     SCARLET:
I have a cop outside my place too, you're not the only one.

     LAURA:
My life was going along just fine.

     SCARLET:
What is that supposed to mean?

LAURA:
Why couldn't you just stay away?

SCARLET:
My sister died, I had to come home.

LAURA:
No you didn't. You came back and fucked up all our lives.

SCARLET:
I didn't mean for all this to happen.

LAURA:
You sure you're not part of it?

SCARLET:
No, I'm not.

LAURA:
I think the cops are looking in the wrong place.

SCARLET;
I had nothing to do with any of this.

LAURA:
I don't believe you.

SCARLET:
Why would I go around killing all my friends?

LAURA;
You were always a bit of an outsider, especially since you took off to college. You left us and then suddenly came back.

SCARLET:
What are you suggesting?

LAURA:
I don't know, but I still think you did it.

SCARLET:
That's crazy.

LAURA:
Is it?

SCARLET:
(angrily)
Then go talk to the police if you think this is true.

LAURA:
I did, they just told me to go home.

SCARLET:
You're just scared.

LAURA:
Damn right I am.

SCARLET:
So am I.

LAURA:
You're lying.

SCARLET:
I am not.

LAURA:
You can fake the anger and the tears but you can't fake it to me.

SCARLET:
(crying)
I'm sorry you feel that way. I guess I'll leave you alone.

LAURA:
I never want to see you again. Just stay away from me.

SCARLET:
If that's what you want.

LAURA:
What I want is my friends back, but you took them from me.

SCARLET:
No I didn't.

LAURA:
Yes you did.

SCARLET:
I'm not going to sit here and listen to this.

LAURA:
Then just leave, like when you left for college.

SCARLET:
Goodbye, Laura.

LAURA:
I'm not even going to say anything to you. I hope you die.

Scarlet starts crying and gets up and leaves.

EXT. - STREET IN FRONT OF COFFEE SHOP – DAY

Scarlet runs outside the coffee shop and gets into her car. The Stalker stands up when Scarlet's car pulls out and he walks into the coffee shop.

INT. - COFFEE SHOP – DAY

Laura is crying at the table when only Stalkers legs walk up.

STALKER (V.O.):
Hey.

LAURA:
Oh hey, what are you doing here?

EXT. - MOM'S HOUSE – DAY

Scarlet's car pulls into the driveway and Scarlet gets out frantically and goes inside. A pair of legs are seen across the street. They start walking towards the house and it turns out to be Jeremy.

BORED COP:
Hey.

JEREMY:
Yeah?

BORED COP:
You can't go up there.

JEREMY:
Why not?

BORED COP:
Only certain people can.

JEREMY:
I'm a friend of Scarlet's.

BORED COP:
Can I see some I.D.?

JEREMY:
Sure.

Jeremy hands the cop some I.D.

BORED COP:
Sorry your name isn't on the list.

JEREMY:
What?

BORED COP:
In fact, she doesn't want you anywhere near her.

JEREMY:
But I really need to talk to her.

BORED COP:
Sorry buddy, there's nothing I can do for you.

JEREMY:
How about if you're there?

BORED COP:
What do you mean?

JEREMY:
That way nothing can happen. She'll be protected the entire time.

BORED COP:
Sure just give me a minute.

Bored Cop picks up his cellphone and pushes a button.

Stalker

BORED COP:
(into cellphone)
Hello, Scarlet?
(pause)
Yes, I got someone out here who wants to talk to you.
(pause)
It's Jeremy.
(pause)
I realize that, but he said I can stick around.
(pause)
Alright, see ya in a few.
(to Jeremy)
She's on her way out.

JEREMY:
Thank you.

BORED COP:
Just behave.

Scarlet walks out of the house looking angry. The Bored Cop leans on his car and waits. Jeremy looks nervous.

SCARLET:
(angrily)
What are you doing here?

JEREMY:
I just wanted to talk to you.

SCARLET:
You should confess to the police.

JEREMY:
I didn't do anything.

SCARLET:
Yes, you did.

JEREMY:
Honestly.

SCARLET:
Now because of you, my friends are abandoning me. Haven't you had your fill?

JEREMY:
I don't know what to say to make you realize it wasn't me.

SCARLET:
Because it was you.

JEREMY:
I came here to try and explain to you that it wasn't, I can see that was pointless.

Jeremy starts to walk off.

SCARLET:
(yelling)
Just come clean you freak.

Scarlet storms off back into the house.

INT. - MOM'S LIVING ROOM – DAY

BRADY:
What did he want?

SCARLET:
To try and tell me it wasn't him.

BRADY:
Did he try to explain anything?

SCARLET:
No, I just started yelling at him and he walked off.

BRADY:
That's for the best.

SCARLET:
I just want him caught.

BRADY:
I'm sure he will be.

SCARLET:
He better be.

EXT. - JOHN'S HOUSE – NIGHT

Friendly Detective walks up to John's front door and knocks. When the door opens DRUNK MOM answers the door.

DRUNK MOM:
Well, looky what we have here.

FRIENDLY DETECTIVE:
I'm looking for John.

DRUNK MOM:
John? Did you get me a stripper?

JOHN (V.O.):
No mom.

DRUNK MOM:
Damn. Then what did you want?

FRIENDLY DETECTIVE:
I want to talk to John.

DRUNK MOM:
You sure?

FRIENDLY DETECTIVE:
Yes please.

DRUNK MOM:
Fine.
(yelling)
John, it's for you.

JOHN (V.O.):
Who is it?

Stalker

DRUNK MOM:
I think it's a cop.

> *John comes running up to the front door.*

JOHN:
Can I help you?

FRIENDLY DETECTIVE:
I would like to ask you some questions about the string of recent deaths.

JOHN:
Sure, anything I can do to help.
(to Drunk Mom)
Mom, go sit down.

> *Drunk Mom goes into the house.*

FRIENDLY DETECTIVE:
Is this a bad time?

JOHN:
No, this is typical mom. Don't worry about it.

FRIENDLY DETECTIVE:
I'm sorry.

JOHN:
It's fine, whatever.

FRIENDLY DETECTIVE:
We've discovered you had quite a bit of history with some of the girls involved in all this.

JOHN:
Yeah, I dated Jamie.

FRIENDLY DETECTIVE:
What about the sister of the first girl, Sara?

JOHN:
Scarlet? Yeah, we used to date. What about it?

FRIENDLY DETECTIVE:
Any lingering feelings for her that you were aware of?

JOHN:
No, I was in love with Jamie.

FRIENDLY DETECTIVE:
Are you sure?

JOHN:
Yeah, I'm sure.

> *John leans in to a table. Friendly Detective takes a defensive stance. John pulls out a ring box.*

JOHN:
Relax, it's just an engagement ring. I was going to ask Jamie to marry me.

FRIENDLY DETECTIVE:
Seems you were pretty serious.

JOHN:
We were.

FRIENDLY DETECTIVE:
How hard did you take her death?

JOHN:
It was surprising. Once she died though I started having my suspicions about Jeremy.

FRIENDLY DETECTIVE:
Why Jeremy?

JOHN:
In high school he was madly in love with Scarlet, stalked her and everything.

FRIENDLY DETECTIVE:
That's a pretty serious accusation.

JOHN:
It's the truth though.

FRIENDLY DETECTIVE:
How does his past relate to what's been happening?

JOHN:
I dunno, but it makes the most sense.

FRIENDLY DETECTIVE:
Okay, well thanks for talking to me.

JOHN:
Hey no problem.

Friendly Detective walks back to his car.

INT. - JOHN'S HOUSE – NIGHT

John closes the door. The inside of the house is a dump. Garbage lays all over the place and there are holes in the furniture. Drunk Mom is sitting in a chair with flies buzzing around it.

DRUNK MOM:
What did the pigs want?

JOHN:
Nothing to worry about.

DRUNK MOM:
Now that Jamie left, maybe you can go back after that Scarlet.

JOHN:
Maybe mom.

DRUNK MOM:
Where did Jamie go anyway?

JOHN:
I'm not sure, she said she'd call though.

DRUNK MOM:
I never liked her, you can do better.

JOHN:
Okay, mom.

INT. - MOM'S LIVING ROOM – NIGHT

Someone knocks on the door and Mom walks up and answers it. Laura is standing on the other side.

MOM:
Laura, it's been a long time, how've you been?

LAURA:
Before lately, pretty good.

MOM:
I know, I'm so sorry.

LAURA:
It's okay, I'll set everything straight soon.

MOM:
What's your plan?

LAURA:
I'm keeping that to myself.

MOM:
Okay, how can I help you?

LAURA:
Is Scarlet home?

MOM:
Yeah she is.
(into house)
Scarlet, it's for you.

Scarlet walks up to the front door.

SCARLET:
(surprised)
Laura. What are you doing here?

LAURA:
I thought we should talk.

SCARLET:
Are you still mad at me?

LAURA:
Not really. I think I'm just more mad at what's happening.

SCARLET:
Did you want to come in?

LAURA:
No, can we go for a walk?

SCARLET:
Sure.

MOM:
I wouldn't honey.

SCARLET:
I trust Laura.

MOM:
It's not Laura I'm worried about.

SCARLET:
I won't be gone long.

MOM:
That's all it could take.

LAURA:
I'll take good care of Scarlet.

SCARLET:
See Mom? I'll be fine.

MOM:
Alright, but I don't like this.

SCARLET:
You don't even like me leaving the house.

MOM:
Can you blame me?

Scarlet puts on a jacket.

SCARLET:
I'll be back soon.

MOM:
Alright.

Mom closes the door.

EXT. - STREET IN FRONT OF MOM'S – NIGHT

Scarlet and Laura walk off down the drive way and Scarlet walks up to the Bored Cop.

SCARLET:
Just so you know, I'm going for a quick walk with her.

BORED COP:
I wouldn't suggest that.

SCARLET:
I'll be fine.

BORED COP:
Don't go far.

SCARLET:
I won't, I promise.

Scarlet rejoins Laura and they walk down the street.

Stalker

SCARLET:
I'm glad you came. The way we left things was really bothering me.

LAURA:
Yeah, same here.

SCARLET:
What did you do after I left?

LAURA:
Oh, a friend came and talked with me for a bit.

SCARLET:
Which friend?

LAURA:
Someone you wouldn't know.

SCARLET:
Ah, I see.

LAURA:
You girls may have been my closest friends, but you weren't my only friends.

SCARLET:
Yeah, that's true.

LAURA:
He helped me to see reason.

SCARLET:
He must have been pretty convincing, you were pretty upset when I left.

LAURA:
He managed to calm me down. Made me realize that I'm the only one that can solve my own issues.

SCARLET:
How so?

LAURA:
Well, I can sit around and do nothing, which would make me all depressed. The other option is to get out and do something and try to get passed it.

SCARLET:
Sounds like good advice.

LAURA:
Yeah, I thought so.

SCARLET:
Did he give you any ideas of what to do?

LAURA:
Yeah, some.

SCARLET:
What did he suggest?

LAURA:
That I should get away for a bit.

SCARLET:
That's what Jamie did and look what happened to her.

LAURA:
I know, but I'm not going to just leave like she did.

SCARLET:
Then what else are you going to do?

LAURA:
I figured I'd deal with the whole situation once and for all and then leave.

SCARLET:
How are you going to do that.

Laura reaches into her purse and pulls out a gun.

SCARLET:
Whoa, what are you doing?

LAURA:
Dealing with the situation.

SCARLET:
What?

Laura points the gun at Scarlet.

LAURA:
Before you come and hunt me down like you did Jamie, I'm going to get you off my tail first.

SCARLET:
(frantically)
I swear it wasn't me.

LAURA:
I still don't believe your lies.

SCARLET:
I'm not a liar.

LAURA:
Shut up. I don't want to hear it.

Laura points the gun and fires. The gun kicks up in Laura's hand and Scarlet ducks. The bullet doesn't hit Scarlet.

SCARLET:
Okay, calm down. Killing me won't solve anything.

LAURA:
It will solve everything.

SCARLET:
If you kill me, the cops will arrest you.

LAURA:
At least I'll get vengeance.

SCARLET:
This isn't the way to deal with this.

LAURA:
Yes, it is.

Laura points the gun up at Scarlet again. Just before she fires, Laura's chest explodes in a bloody, gory mess. Scarlet screams as some gore sprays on her. The Bored Cop comes running up after Laura slumps into the street.

BORED COP:
Are you okay?

SCARLET:
(crying)
Yes, thank you.

BORED COP:
Hey, no problem.

SCARLET:
How'd you know?

BORED COP:
I just didn't like the look of it.

Scarlet collapses to the sidewalk, crying. Stalker's dark shadow is seen down the street walking off.

Act 5

INT. - MOM'S LIVING ROOM – NIGHT

The front door opens and Scarlet is being helped in by Bored Cop.

MOM:
What happened?

BORED COP:
That girl tried to kill her.

MOM:
What?

BRADY:
What?

SCARLET:
She blamed me for all the deaths. Said she'd kill me for revenge.

MOM:
That's crazy.

BORED COP:
I'm going to check around outside.

MOM:
Okay.

The Bored Cop leaves and closes the door.

SCARLET:
I can't keep dealing with all this.

BRADY:
It'll be over soon.

SCARLET:
None of my close friends are alive, they've all been killed.

BRADY:
I think we should call that detective.

MOM:
I'm sure that cop outside has already told him.

BRADY:
Yeah, probably.

Brady hugs Scarlet. Scarlet cries into his arms.

BRADY:
We'll be okay. I promise.

Stalker
INT. - JOHN'S HOUSE – NIGHT

> *Drunk Mom is sitting in her chair unconscious. The TV is on and blaring. Stalker walks into the house and stands in the living room. Mom wakes up.*

DRUNK MOM:
Who are you?

STALKER:
A friend.

DRUNK MOM:
A friend would bring me some vodka.

STALKER:
I got something better.

DRUNK MOM:
Ooh, what's it called?

> *Stalker pulls out a knife.*

DRUNK MOM:
I don't get it.

STALKER:
You weren't always like this. When your lover left you alone with your son, you changed and became the alcoholic are now.

DRUNK MOM:
I was so sad when he left, I didn't know what else to do.

STALKER:
Your son needed you.

DRUNK MOM:
I did my best.

STALKER:
It wasn't enough.

> *Stalker stabs Drunk Mom. She gurgles up some blood and then dies.*

STALKER:
Bitch.

> *Stalker spits on her body then leaves the house.*

EXT. - MOM'S HOUSE – NIGHT

> *The Bored Cop is sitting in the car listening to the radio. His notebook is laying open on the seat beside him and the occasional white noise is heard on the radio. A shadow descends on the Bored Cop. He looks at the shadow, it is John.*

BORED COP:
Can I help you?

JOHN:
Yeah, I want to talk to Scarlet.

BORED COP:
I wouldn't suggest that right now.

JOHN:
Why not?

BORED COP:
She's had a pretty rough night.

JOHN:
I'll be gentle, I promise.

BORED COP:
I still don't suggest it.

JOHN:
It'll only take a second.

BORED COP:
Alright, fine. Go, just be quick.

JOHN:
I will, thanks.

John walks away from the cop car and to the front door and knocks.

INT. - MOM'S LIVING ROOM – NIGHT

MOM:
Who could that be at this time of night?

SCARLET:
I have no idea.

Scarlet runs up and answers the door, John smiles when the door opens.

SCARLET:
John, what are you doing here?

JOHN:
Just came by to see if you were alright.

SCARLET:
Yeah, how'd you know?

JOHN:
A cop stopped by my place to tell me about Laura.

Scarlet starts to cry.

JOHN:
Hey, I'm sorry.

SCARLET:
Sorry, this is just a little awkward.

JOHN:
I know, the whole "we used to date" thing, but it's all good.

SCARLET:
You sure?

JOHN:
Sure I am. If I wasn't I wouldn't be here. I'm not Jeremy after all.

Stalker
>   *Scarlet laughs.*

SCARLET:
Yeah, you got a point. You wanna come in?

JOHN:
Sure.

>   *John walks in and sees Mom and Brady sitting in the living room.*

JOHN:
Hey, what's up?

BRADY:
John, right?

JOHN:
Yeah, that's right.

MOM:
I haven't seen you since, well, since you know.

JOHN:
It's all good. I heard about Laura and wanted to make sure she was okay.

MOM:
Well that's nice.

>   *John looks around and sees some suitcases packed.*

JOHN:
Going somewhere?

SCARLET:
Yeah, we were heading back to campus.

JOHN:
How come?

SCARLET:
Laura was a bit to close to home, so we're getting out of here.

JOHN:
Good plan.

SCARLET:
We thought so.

>   *Brady walks up to John.*

BRADY:
We were going to head out in a few minutes. So please, make it quick.

JOHN:
Sure, I won't be long.

SCARLET:
Is there something else?

JOHN:
Yeah, there is.

John pulls out a knife and stabs Brady. Brady tries to pull the knife out, but John holds it in place. Brady tries to scream out but John twists the blade and Brady falls down dead.

SCARLET:
What the hell?

Mom sees what's going on and screams. She starts waving her arms in front of the living room window.

JOHN/STALKER:
I wouldn't do that.

MOM:
(screaming)
Please help us.

John runs up, covers Mom's mouth and begins stabbing her. He stabs her multiple times and blood spread over the front window. Scarlet looks on in horror. John walks up and locks the front door.

SCARLET:
I don't understand.

JOHN/STALKER:
What's there not to understand?

SCARLET:
Why are you doing this?

JOHN/STALKER:
Remember when we were kids in high school?

SCARLET:
Yeah, of course.

JOHN/STALKER:
We all made a promise to each other. We'd all never change and would stay friends forever.

SCARLET:
It was a foolish promise, everybody changes.

JOHN/STALKER:
Not me, I haven't changed.

SCARLET:
So what did my sister have to do with this?

JOHN/STALKER:
She was a decoy.

SCARLET:
Excuse me?

JOHN/STALKER:
I needed a way to get you home. So I killed her.

SCARLET:
What about Cynthia, and Jamie?

JOHN/STALKER:
Cynthia became a dyke and Jamie wasn't the flirtatious and trampy girl that she was.

Stalker

SCARLET:
You're sick.

JOHN/STALKER:
That's what my psychiatrist said.

SCARLET:
And what happened to him?

JOHN/STALKER:
I think you know.

SCARLET:
What do you want from me? How did I change?

JOHN/STALKER:
I wanted you. I used to respect you. But then your parents split and you started putting out. I should have had that, I wanted you so bad but I held back. Then you went off to school and I couldn't get you. Now, you're here and I'm going to take what I should have had all those years ago.

SCARLET:
I'm not going to let you rape me.

JOHN/STALKER:
I'm not giving you an option.

SCARLET:
Please no.

The door starts to bang.

JOHN/STALKER:
Shit.

John/Stalker ducks into the kitchen. The door bursts open and Bored Cop comes in with his gun drawn.

SCARLET:
(screaming)
He's in the kitchen.

BORED COP:
Get out of here.

SCARLET:
I can't.

BORED COP:
Do it, now.

Bored Cop waves for Scarlet to run past him. Scarlet runs but John/Stalker grabs at her. The cop fires his gun but the back window in the kitchen blasts out. John/Stalker wrestles with the cop.

BORED COP:
Run.

Scarlet starts to run for the front door when John/Stalker pulls his knife and stabs it into the Bored Cop's neck. The Bored Cop gurgles, blood flows out of his neck and he dies. Scarlet starts to run out of the house and John/Stalker chases her.

EXT. - MOM'S HOUSE - NIGHT

JOHN/STALKER:
Come here you whore.

John/Stalker catches up with her and drags her to the ground. She tries to fight with him to get herself free but he manages to pull her back into the house.

INT. - MOM'S LIVING ROOM - NIGHT

He throws her on the living room floor beside her dead mom.

SCARLET:
Please don't do this.

JOHN/STALKER:
You should have given yourself to me all those years ago.

SCARLET:
Please I beg you.

John/Stalker reaches down and rips off her shirt revealing her bra. Scarlet kicks her leg and nails him right in the nuts. He crumples over and starts to scream.

JOHN/STALKER:
You bitch.

Scarlet tries to get to the front door but John/Stalker is in the way. He grabs onto her leg as she tries to run by. Scarlet falls to the floor.

JOHN/STALKER:
You're not going anywhere.

John/Stalker puts his hand over her mouth. Scarlet tries to scream but can't be heard. John/Stalker smiles but is suddenly pulled off her onto his back. Jeremy is standing there.

SCARLET:
(screaming)
Help me.

JOHN/STALKER:
Oh, look, the original stalker.

JEREMY:
That was a long time ago.

JOHN/STALKER:
C'mon admit it. You want her. Join me, we can do this together.

JEREMY:
You're demented. It's not going to happen.

JOHN/STALKER:
You can have everything you dreamed of.

SCARLET:
Please don't.

JEREMY:
No, I won't.

John/Stalker readies his knife.

Stalker

JOHN/STALKER:
Fine, be difficult.

John/Stalker lunges at Jeremy and Jeremy wrestles him. Scarlet curls into a ball at the far side of the living room. She starts to cry as they fight.

JOHN/STALKER:
Aww, look at that, you made her cry.

JEREMY:
Shut up.

JOHN/STALKER:
You can still have her.

JEREMY:
I was always jealous of you in high school. You had her, but now, now you're just mental.

JOHN/STALKER:
(laughs)
Oh, I'm hurt.

John/Stalker lunges again and manages to stab Jeremy. Scarlet screams as Jeremy slumps to the floor.

JOHN/STALKER:
Now that that's done with.

SCARLET:
Please, if you leave, I promise I won't tell anybody.

JOHN/STALKER:
You seem to be missing the point of all this.

SCARLET:
Please don't hurt me.

JOHN/STALKER:
Oh, I'm gonna make you scream.

A gun shot is heard and John/Stalker suddenly stops. He turns around to face Jeremy and Jeremy is holding the cops smoking gun. A bullet hole is in John/Stalker's back.

JOHN/STALKER:
What the?

Jeremy fires twice more. John/Stalker manages to stay standing and runs for Jeremy. Jeremy keeps firing till the gun clicks. John/Stalker lunges at Jeremy but just manages to fall on him. Scarlet runs over and sees neither moving.

SCARLET:
Jeremy, are you okay?

A moan is heard. Scarlet rolls John/Stalker off of Jeremy and Jeremy is seen holding his stab wound.

SCARLET:
Good your still alive.

JEREMY:
I'm sorry this all happened.

SCARLET:
It's okay, why were you here again?

JEREMY:
(groaning)
I came to try and say sorry and that I wouldn't bother you again.

SCARLET:
I thought I scared you off.

JEREMY:
You did, but I had to try again.

SCARLET:
Why?

JEREMY:
I couldn't bear the thought of you being mad at me.

SCARLET:
You still have feelings for me, don't you?

JEREMY:
Yes, I do.

SCARLET:
You'll be okay, we'll get you out of here.

Friendly Detective comes in the front door.

FRIENDLY DETECTIVE:
What happened?

SCARLET:
It was John, this whole time.

FRIENDLY DETECTIVE:
Damn.

SCARLET:
What are you doing here?

FRIENDLY DETECTIVE:
I stopped by John's house again, and his mom had been stabbed to death. I thought I'd come back here and make sure you were alright.

SCARLET:
I am now.

FRIENDLY DETECTIVE:
(points at Jeremy)
Did he save you?

SCARLET:
Yeah he did.

FRIENDLY DETECTIVE:
Alright son, let's get you some help.

Stalker
EXT. - SERENE CEMETARY – DAY

A group of people are standing around a gravestone. The Sad Minister closes his bible and people start to clear away. Scarlet remains standing there for a few moments. Jeremy comes up behind her.

JEREMY:
Hey, how was it?

SCARLET:
It was sad, how was Laura's service?

JEREMY:
Not a lot of people showed up.

SCARLET:
Why not?

JEREMY:
I figured all her friends are dead and the one that isn't she tried to kill.

SCARLET
Yeah true.

JEREMY:
You glad this is all over?

SCARLET:
Yeah, but so many people had to die.

JEREMY:
I'm sure they're looking down on us.

SCARLET:
You really think so?

JEREMY:
I know so.

SCARLET:
Thank you.

JEREMY:
For what?

SCARLET:
For being here.

JEREMY:
It's not a problem.

SCARLET:
You really didn't know my mom though.

JEREMY:
Yeah, but you needed someone here with you.

SCARLET:
Sorry, I judged you so harshly.

JEREMY:
You needed to take your anger out on someone.

SCARLET:
That doesn't excuse what I said and did.

JEREMY:
It's over now, so no worries.
(pause)
You hear from the police at all?

SCARLET:
Yeah, the detective that was handling the case said that when they searched John's house they found entire murals of me and journals about what he was going to do.

JEREMY:
Creepy.

SCARLET:
I just never imagined it would be him.

JEREMY:
Did you ever love him?

SCARLET:
No, he was just a fling. That was why I dumped him all those years ago.

JEREMY:
Would he have got what he wanted if your parents broke up sooner?

SCARLET:
Probably.

JEREMY:
Just bad timing then I guess.

SCARLET:
I suppose you could look at it that way.

Dad pulls up in a car. He rolls down the window and leans out.

DAD:
You ready to go?

SCARLET:
Yeah, I guess.

JEREMY:
Before you go I was wondering, would you ever want to go out for coffee with me?

SCARLET:
(shocked)
Umm, maybe, I'll let you know.

JEREMY:
(sadly)
Oh, okay.

SCARLET:
Just let me figure this all out alright?

JEREMY:
Sure.

Scarlet kisses Jeremy on the cheek.

Stalker

SCARLET:
Good-bye, Jeremy.

JEREMY:
Bye, Scarlet.

Scarlet gets in Dad's car and the car pulls away. Jeremy stands looking down at Mom's grave. He suddenly tightens his fists and looks angry as the car pulls away.